Anonymous

A Letter to the People of Great Britain

on the present alarming crisis

Anonymous

A Letter to the People of Great Britain
on the present alarming crisis

ISBN/EAN: 9783337380977

Printed in Europe, USA, Canada, Australia, Japan

Cover: Foto ©Andreas Hilbeck / pixelio.de

More available books at **www.hansebooks.com**

✕✕✕✕✕✕✕✕✕✕✕✕✕✕✕✕✕✕✕✕

A
LETTER

TO THE

PEOPLE of GREAT BRITAIN,

ON

The prefent alarming CRISIS.

✕✕✕✕✕✕✕✕✕✕✕✕✕✕✕✕✕✕✕✕

[Price One Shilling and Six-pence.]

A

LETTER

TO THE

PEOPLE of GREAT BRITAIN,

ON

The prefent alarming Crisis.

Pointing at the moft eligible Means

For limiting the Number of PLACE-MEN
and PENSIONERS, in Parliament,

And putting an End to

BRIBERY AND CORRUPTION;

To obviate the DANGERS which now threaten
this KINGDOM.

LONDON:

Sold at Mr. *Dodfley's*, *Pall-Mall*; Mr. *Davis's* and Mr. *Al-mon's*, in *Piccadilly*; Mr. *Hall's*, in *Gerrard-ftreet*, *Soho*; Mr. *Hutchinfon's*, in *Piccadilly*; Mr. *Bingley's*, *Newgate-ftreet*; Mr. *Williams's*, *Fleet-ftreet*; Mr *Anderfon's*, St. *Paul's Church-yard*; Meffrs *Richardfon* and *Urquhart*, *Royal Exchange*; the Bockfellers about *Charing Crofs* and *Weftminfter-Hall*, and moft Pamphlet Shops in Town.

M DCC LXXI.

A

LETTER

TO THE

PEOPLE of GREAT BRITAIN,

ON

The prefent alarming C R I S I S.

Friends and Countrymen,

YOU have had for a long time fre-
quent warnings, that your excef-
five corruption was leading your country
to approaching ruin : the grand criterion
is now, I fear, at length, arrived ; for
by the great number of *falfe patriots* you
have had for fome years paſt to manage
public affairs, pretending the good of the
common weal in conducting your *national
interefts*, whilſt their own emoluments
alone were the primary objects of occu-
pation in their miniſtry, they have treat-

B   ed

ed you with deceit: and inftead of changing meafures, have only chang'd hands to complete the impious fcheme; leaving a broken *confiitution* ready to fall into the hands of the *common enemy*, to finifh a work of *flavery*, for you and your *children* to inherit.

In order to clear up this point beyond a doubt, it becomes neceffary to form a a little retrofpection, and to lay before you a fhort narrative of thofe *celebrated patriotic minifiers*, who, in the beginning, erected the iniquitous bafis of this deftructive plan: for which purpofe I fhall date the melancholy æra from the traiterous and *inglorious peace of Utrecht.*

Our *patriotic minifters* of that day, fold to *old Lewis* what his *powerful armies* cou'd not, and were not able to atchieve by the *fword*, viz. a fuperiority over *Great Britain* in her councils and conquefts, as well as thofe of her *allies*, by which the flood gates of corruption were opened, that have fince, like a torrent,

over-

overflowed our *flate* in all our negociations.

In this *infamous peace* was laid the
foundation of that project which was
formed by our patriotic minifters, in
concert with thofe of France and Spain,
to place the Pretender on the throne of
England, by an invafion from the latter,
affifted by the former of thefe two powers, the execution of which was provi-
dentially retarded for fome time, by the
death of the Queen, though it took place
the year following, by the Earl of Mar's
raifing a rebellion in Scotland, and the
Pretender's landing there foon after, with
fome Spanifh troops; but the death of
old Lewis, and the wife and prudent
meafures of his then gracious majefty
George the Firft, in cultivating a friendfhip, and preferving a good correfpon-
dence with the late Duke of Orleans,
who had prevented feveral other embark-
ations intended to be made in the Pretender's favour; the whole fcheme, by
thefe means, and the bravery of the

Englifh

Englifh troops, who march'd to fight the rebels and their friends the haughty Spaniards, was happily rendered abortive, and the Pretender forced to fly in a greater hurry than he came. Whether the confequences of our late ignominious p—e, with thofe of a more fcandalous and difhonourable convention, if poffible, may not, at a convenient opportunity, produce the fame or worfe effects, as our enemies are now more powerful, and more firmly united than at the above period, every rational man may guefs, if he will not judge, till time and a woeful experience convinces. Thefe, however, were then the works of our patriot minifters, under the foul influence of *French* and *Spanifh* corruption, in whofe courts one of the delinquents, after flying his country, found a fafe afylum and fplendid retreat, being appointed Secretary to this very Pretender, who had previoufly taken the oaths to oppofe; a little time will fhew whether the fame policy is not now on foot.

Our

Our next great *patriot* was the grand corrupter, whofe wifdom never extended to the leaft political idea of any *foreign court :* and who, for want of fpirit, was never able to treat with our enemies upon equal footing.

This *grand financiering patriot,* by a long courfe of mal-ad————n both at home and abroad, rendered you the contempt of France, Spain, and all the foreign powers. His peculiar talent was only in a modern way of corruption, by his fingular art of financiering; that is to fay, in finding out the intrinfic price of every individual that oppofed his corrupt meafures, in preventing his accefs to any *venal boroughs.*

He artfully concluded his bargains on your General Elections, to bring fuch reprefentatives into parliament as were ready to proftitute their votes with their honour, according as he fhould dictate ; for which the public money was lavifh'd with profufion; and having thus corrupted

rupted both conſtituents and repreſentatives, he ſettled a majority of *placemen*
and *penſioners* in your parliaments, to
chain and yoke their own poſterity and
you.

Seeds of jealouſies and diviſions he effectually ſow'd between king and people,
the conſequences of which had been fatal to the nation, if they had not been
·timely perceived and prevented, by our
then moſt *gracious Sovereign*.

The corrupter, however, to crown his
odious ſchemes, loaded your country
with an innumerable hoſt of exciſemen,
and other revenue officers, totally unne-
ceſſary, unleſs to gain votes at elections:
he negociated the *famous Convention*
with *Spain*, and then by his *bribery* ob-
tained an uncontroulable power in government, by which he eſcaped the pu-
niſhment due to theſe inglorious and un-
conſtitutional practices.

He lifted himſelf up amongſt his peers,
and

and left you his prophecy, that when your national debt fhould amount to an hundred millions, you would begin to dwindle, and fall into fuch a degeneracy, that fome weak and imperious minifter would make you flaves, or elfe that you would become a *province* to your *neighbours*.

Oh, *Britons!* examine yourfelves, if the day is far off; and weigh in the fcales of bribery, perjury, and corruption, the *bleffings* this great patriot has left you for a legacy; whofe adminiftration and whofe memory ought to be detefted by every honeft Englifhman, who is defirous or ambitious to fee our laws, and the glorious conftitution of his country, with his own freedom and independence, pure and untainted by fuch atrocious meafures.

I now come to the next junto: A fet of patriotic minifters of the fame ftamp; wherein I fhall only dwell on the Two Brothers, as having the chief lead in this

ad——n

ad——n for a much longer time than was of any fervice to your country.

Common fenfe, honefty, and rational underftanding, blended with fome political knowledge of our national interefts, were neceffary, at this juncture, to retrieve the errors and reform the pernicious fchemes of the two former ad——s.

The Two Brothers were efteemed men of parts, and true-born Englifhmen; but, alas! How frail is human nature! How weak and depraved their endeavours to remedy thefe evils!

France and Spain play'd their old game with them; at one period cajoling, at another, intimidating, and, at a third, cozening: thus, in this round, the political wheel turn'd, whilft our loving Brothers conducted the war with fuch fupinenefs and pufillanimity, that they brought difhonour on a late Englifh Prince, who lov'd his country; facrificed him, the Queen of Hungary, and our allies,

lies, to the ambitious views of our enemies, and committed other fatal blun-
ders too many to enumerate; boldly ad-
vancing and encreasing the schemes of
corruption, which had been bequeathed
them by their predeceffors in ad----n.

They had, however, a tolerable knowledge to *tax you at home*, though very
bad negociators in our national affairs
abroad: As a fpecimen of this fact, they
fhewed you their fkill and judgment,
by the moft infamous treaty of Aix la
Chapelle, where they fent a minifter, who
agreed to give up Cape Breton to our
enemies, the taking of which, in 1749,
by Sir Peter Warren, had coft the nation more than fufficient purchafe, by
blood and treafure: and again, in 1758,
much more to retake it, by our fleets and
armies, under the command of Admiral
Bofcawen and General Amherft; then
tack'd two notable hoftages for payment
of their ignorant and corrupt meafures;
and, left they fhould not be fufficiently
confpicuous on the event of that difho-

C   nourable

nourable and ignoble work, they erected
a magnificent fire-work, which coft the
nation an immenfe fum, to elucidate the
greatnefs of their politics, and made
great rejoicings, which only ferved to
render the weaknefs and foily of their
ad——n more vifible; though intended
to impofe on the minds of the people,
and thofe who were fhort-fighted, to the
end that the enquiry they dreaded might
extinguifh with the artificial *blaze*, whilft
our noble pledges remained as prifoners
in the hands of our enemies, vainly de-
ploring the difgrace of their country :
thus, by the rule of their predeceffors,
in having a determin'd majority of place-
men and penfioners, to approve and applaud their *patriotic government*, they
efcaped being called to account for their
iniquitous ad——n, leaving you the
dupes and laughing-ftock of all the
powers on the continent.

Such, my dear countrymen, are the
national advantages, the delicious fruits
which are always to be collected from
the

the indefatigable labours of place-men
and penfioners, in the extenfive field of
corruption; ever devoted to fanctify the
moft enormous crimes of a wicked
ad——n.

The next junto, or coalition of the
like patriotic m——rs, were led by the
celebrated Renard, the inimitable felf-
financer: this junto, by their dreaming
and lethargic heads of ftate, let *Minorca*
be taken, facrific'd an admiral becaufe
you had no navy; or, more properly,
one fo weak that it was not in a condition to act with effect, by which your
enemy did what he pleas'd; whilft in
the unmerited death of a brave man,
* Galliflioniere made a forrowful triumph.

The fyftem of bribery and corruption
was now carried as high as at any time
before, till by fuch bad meafures, many
mifcarriages, and numberlefs neglects,

* The French Admiral.

a ge-

a general outcry put an end to this ob-
noxious ad————n. But Renard took
care, by his places and emoluments, together with his ſkilful art of ſelf-finan-
cizing, to raiſe to himſelf and his family
the greateſt fortune that ever was ſqueez'd
from the public in ſo ſhort a time, without doing one good act for the nation,
and retired at laſt without account; having run to cover behind the T—n.

The ſucceeding ad————n was that
of the great and glorious Pitt, diſtin-
guiſhed in the annals of our enemies for
the many defeats he gave them; as well
as thoſe of Great Britain, by ſaving her
from ruin and worthy relation.

His views, deſigns, and firmneſs, with
an underſtanding and ſecrecy peculiar to
himſelf, retriev'd the ſtrain'd ſinews of
his *bleeding country*, when near expiring.

He ſhew'd his late M——y, who was
juſtly and truly beloved by his people,
(as the preſent æra can teſtify) as well

as his royal father, though both had been at other times deceived by the duplicity of m——rs, what Britons could, and can do for their monarch, when love cemented their valour: and how feeble the dependance muft be of a prince who relies on the affiftance of mercenaries, compared to the affectionate hearts of his faithful people.

He fhew'd foreign powers your weight and ftrength, and made your enemies feel the provok'd refentments of the wrongs they had done us, and wanted ftill to impofe on his country.

He made the two very courts, which had by chicanery and fuperior fkill in politics, outwitted and rendered contemptible in all their treaties, his predeceffors in ad————n, as is vifible by thefe treaties at this day, humble and pliant. Thofe he reduc'd to that neceffity, that they were ready to fign *chart blanche:* and taught all Europe, I may fay the univerfe, to know what the
ftrength

ſtrength and power of a Britiſh monarch and his people can do, when properly managed and exerted, with unanimity exiſting among them, through the honeſt and upright conduct of a popular m——r, independent of the venal voices and falſe applauſe of place-men and penſioners.

But, Britons, how fatal is your bane of corruption! By ſelling your votes to place-men and penſioners, who only buy you to ſell you again, you have given up the noble character of free Britons, ſo much honoured, reſpected and admired in every part of the globe: with this you have created diſtruſt, faction, and danger in the grand C—— of the nation, by returning ſuch infamous r——s.

By theſe betrayers of their c——, of their own honour, and of your confidence, (for I will not ſuppoſe you knew their ſecret, perfidious, mercenary deſigns) you veſted in an ignorant, inſolent, preſumptuous man, who was, unfortunately

fortunately for this nation, brought into public affairs, a power to overturn your *patriot*, in voting a fwarm of place-men and penfioners, at your elections, into par————t, the neceffary auxiliaries for carrying into execution the malevolent defigns of a profligate m————r to ruin your country, and render you flaves to his defpotic rule : loading yourfelves, by this infatuation, with unneceffary taxes, for re-payment of an hundred thoufand times more than you received by intoxication, as the wages of his iniquitous fchemes; the furplus of which, after filling his own coffers, he difpofed of as he thought fit amongft his dependents, or for other evil purpofes, in preparing for a flight from that country where he could not with fafety remain, by the injuries he had done it, and the oppreffions he had laid on the people ; a provifion therefore was neceffary, though at their coft.

To overturn your *patriot*, who had fo often overturned your foreign enemies, and

and reduced them to fubmiffion and beg-
gary, by his wifdom and *patriotic miniftry*, to fave you from ruin, and fupport
your rights, was furely the higheft act of
ingratitude. To pour in a troop of
place-men and penfioners, to diftrefs
him in his good defigns for your benefit,
and to oppofe and opprefs thofe great and
worthy patriots who ftood up, and ftill
ftand forth in defence of your freedom
and liberties, as Englifhmen, one of
whom has been almoft a martyr to mi-
nifterial vengeance, was ftill worfe. Your
patriot never rely'd on, or call'd in place-
men or penfioners, the horrors of his
and every honeft man's mind, to effect
the national glories of his miniftry, to
applaud his actions, or fkreen him from
difgrace and national refentment, if the
fmalleft charge could have been fuggefted
againft his popular meafures, in the pro-
fecution of which, the fmalleft veftige
could not be trac'd by his moft fecret
enemies, as nothing but fuccefs and conquefts attended our fleets and armies
during his upright ad———n.

To

To overturn fuch a patriot, I fay, by fending into p———t fuch a fet as never difgraced more effectually a h---e which fhould be revered for national wifdom, integrity, and refolution, in preferving your rights and liberties, and fupporting and protecting your trade, freedom, and conftitution, againft a tyrannic and over-bearing m———r, could be owing to nothing lefs than the folly and infatuation you were under in being betrayed into this grievous misfortune, by the force of an almoft general corruption : for the accomplifhment of which the *public money*, in other words, your money, was wantonly fquandered to delude and deceive you ; a relation which future ages will hardly believe to be the conduct of true-born Englifhmen : Hence I advife, that you who have finn'd, may fin no more, left your repentance may come too late.

But left this fyftem of bringing place-men and penfioners into your p———s, fhould not anfwer the intended purpofes, or mifcarry in the progrefs of the in-

tended

tended project, of supporting the pernicious views of a wicked m——r, our vi-
gilant enemies, always attentive to every
thing they can improve to their own advantage, and to diftrefs this nation,
added foreign corruption to that which
was domeftic, to root your patriot out,
whofe power and abilities they had felt
and dreaded.

How fimilar, then, was the cafe of
your patriot to that of Sir Walter Ra-
leigh, I leave you to determine : I fhall
only obferve in this place, that the latter
loft his head, after all the fervices he had
rendered his country, by the corruption
of *Spanifh gold*; and your glorious patriot
the power to ferve you, in your being
corrupted with the very money which
your honeft induftry has earn'd in the
fweat of your brow : both thefe actions
muft remain indelible blots on this nation while hiftory endureth, efpecially
that relevant to Sir Walter, which ftains
the Stuarts reign with infamy for ever.

Thus

Thus you have committed a crime against your country which finks her into *ruin*, and is now become the fource of all thofe grievances fo juftly felt by you in thofe diftracted days of difcontent and confufion, and the very foundation of all, the foreign infults this kingdom has lately received and tamely fubmitted to.

It is but part of the punifhment your own conduct has brought upon you, which will never be remedied but by a limitation of *place-men and penfioners* in your future parliaments, with fevere and penal laws to prevent any further corruption.

I fay, from the fall or retirement of your great patriot, who finding his councils over-rul'd, his weight and intereft over-power'd, he was at laft obliged to fubmit to terms, which were, from that fatal period, inglorious to himfelf, and injurious to his country: fince which, your enemies abroad, as well as the fecret betrayers of your rights and liberties

at

at home, have conftantly triumph'd at this unwith'd-for event; as the conquefts and victories of the Britifh arms, under his ad———n, were extended throughout the univerle; by which France was reduced to the loweft extremity, whilft Spain was crowding all the fail fhe could make to the gulph of her own deftruction: but this promifing fcene of future fuccefs was foon chang'd by the weaknefs and treachery of his fucceflors.

No fooner was the power of ferving his country removed from him, than the helm of the ftate was grafp'd by a pilot who knew not his compafs, or the eafy courfe he might fteer to arrive at the Cape of Good Hope in fafety, had he continued the line of direction which his predeceflor had laid down and followed. The naval preparations and other armaments of our enemies, were great and formidable at this time; the fecret of their deftination was well preferved, and an invafion would certainly have taken place, though the event fhould prove

ever

ever fo fatal. The whole was difcovered
to the Premier, and that, in fuch a manner, as enabled him to ruin France for
an age to come. The reward of the important fervice of defeating the danger-
ous enterprize, by difcovering the whole
of the defign, and where the enemy
might be furprized and taken, has been
diftrefs and perfecution, with notorious
fraud, committed by m——l authority
and connivance, on the gentleman who
rendered this great fervice to the nation,
and common juftice deny'd him therein,
of which, I believe, we fhall have fome
very interefting, fingular, and remarka-
ble particulars, on propofitions lately
made to a Lord in ad————n, as it is
not doubted but a virtuous m——y will
fooner or later take place, and redrefs,
in a fhort time, all our grievances. A
coward heart and ignorant head are fel-
dom productive of great events : ingratitude, artifice and meannefs, are the
firft bloffoms that appear when their
power is rooted. Had the Premier of
the day but as much military fkill as a

militia

militia drummer, or as much courage as even a Portuguefe, or the eyes of an owl, by their combination he might, if he had thought fit, affumed on the occafion the motto of Cæfar, with propriety; *Veni, vidi, vici*. Inftead of embracing and purfuing thofe advantages, negociations were fet on foot for a peace: pick and choofe your m——rs was the word, and it was with difficulty any were found to undertake the difagreeable tafk. In your negociations your enemies took the advantage, as they have always done fince the memorable peace firft above-mentioned, and began to play their old pranks: the Spanifh court immediately juggled in their overtures with the Earl of B——l, your ambaffador: Wall, the Spanifh minifter, took up the cudgel, acting the part of the imperious haughty *Don*, and bamboozled your m——rs in their negociations.

Monfieur Nivlenofe, the Bouquet, or fweet-fcented myrtle of Verfailles, in his

.nego-

negociations, amufed our m——s with
fweet words and fine promifes, according to the mode of his country: and at
the entertainments which he gave to the
Englifh m——rs, when thofe fweets did
not well go down, he never failed high-
ly to feafon their ragou's with falt and
vinegar, whilft the chamber was perfu-
med with the odoriferous fmell of gun-
powder or fulphur, by which he gained
his point; making ufe of thefe words a
few days before his departure, on talk-
ing with a gentleman of his own country, after dinner: " *Vous voyez mon cher.*
" *ami que la paix eft faite, Eh bien! les*
" *Anglois fout fichu, ils n'ont que de s'en*
" *prendre à milor B—e.*" " You fee,
" my dear friend, that peace is conclu-
" ded: Well, the Englifh are outwit-
" ted; if they are angry, it muft be with
" Lord B—e." The other contemptu-
ous reprefentations he made of the Englifh nobility, at Verfailles, after his arrival there, notwithftanding their polite-
nefs to him, and the prefents made to
him by many of the firft rank, will be
                                    fhewn

fhewn on another occafion. The French-
man, however, owed moft of thefe fa-
vours to place-men and penfioners.

Such, countrymen, was almoft your
irreparable misfortune, that by the in-
troduction of one man into power, he
immediately form'd a corrupt and pufil-
lanimous m——y, that gave the finifh-
ing ftroke to the moft glorious æra of
the Britifh annals, by patching up the
moft infamous, fcandalous, and inglorious p—e that ever was fram'd, made,
or concluded by the weakeft capacities
of men, or corrupt beings of human nature; almoft equal to delivering you into
the hands of the common enemy, whofe
continued labours have been fince that
day, and are actually now employed in
forging chains for you, to confummate
their fcheme of tyranny and oppreffion
over a once brave and free people.

The peace-maker, though convinced
that his odious p---e would be damn'd
by all the honeft and independent of the
king-

kingdom, had neverthelefs the art to get
it applauded by a majority of place-men
and penfioners; but unable to withftand
the refentments and outcries of an en-
rag'd and injur'd people, for this auda-
cious impofition, he foon after thought
fit to decamp, leaving his auxiliaries to
fupport the infamous p—e, to which
they had given their higheft approbation,
and by which they had rendered themfelves the abomination of their country.

Oh, *Havannah! Havannah! Blood of
Britons! Key* to the riches and command
of all the Spanifh territories in *North*
and *South America*, How art thou loft?
and for what?

Oh, Banks of Newfoundland! Thy
fifheries how neceffary to be preferved,
thy coafts kept facred, and no loop-holes
left for thy falfe, perfidious enemy to
create new quarrels; why not facred?
and for what expofed and left open?
unlefs to tempt the enemy to enter and
poffefs this invaluable appendage to the

E　　　　Britifh

Britiſh crown. What had the enemy to
return for the conqueſt of Pondicherry,
equal to the expence of the blood and trea-
ſure expended to make it ours? Infatuated
Britons! all this is left unpuniſh'd: Why,
Britons? by your own venality; for your
enemies might have been obliged to have
ceded to you the conqueſts your arms
had won, paid you the expences of the
war, and thank'd you for any peace that
might be granted them on your own
terms; had not treachery and cowardice
betray'd your rights, whilſt corruption
prevail'd in your councils and ſenate.

Thus far has the blood, the conqueſts
and riches of Great Britain been given up
by your judicious and ſkilful negociators. Examine now what relief of taxes
your peace has produced, what advantages or glory redounded to the nation,
from this ignominious tranſaction, and
what encreaſe of revenue, trade, wealth,
or honour, has been accumulated for our
king and country, from that period to
the preſent time. As to my own part,

I know

I know of none; but this I know, that many impolitic meafures have been the daily practice to accomplifh your *ruin*, which are vifible to all, except to thofe who have fold their honour and their country for places or penfions, and fuch as depend upon them; as there are none fo blind as thofe who will not fee.

Without any good effect, we have had juntos upon juntos of m——s ignorant of their departments. When a few of the noble and fteady friends of the conftitution, and your common interefts, came into play, they were foon difmiffed for oppofing thofe meafures that tended to your ruin, by an execrated leader.

Coalitions upon coalitions we have feen attempted upon the fame plan; *ins* and *outs* innumerable we have all feen, to compleat the breaches ignorance or defign has created, in negociations and unconftitutional rule of government; labouring with unfuccefsful c.. ..rs

E 2   to

to fmother the general and continued
outcries againft corruption. Blefs'd with
fuch a leader and his partifans, you are
furely arrived at the higheft pitch of
earthly happinefs, as in none of thefe
changes any endeavour could prevail to
change the pernicious fyftem for our
downfal, to impeach defaulters, or point
out the means for national redrefs or relief, though the complaints of an inju-
red and oppreffed people have never
ceas'd to require it.

From the detefted p—e, you are already arrived to the eve of a war, unlefs
prevented for a few weeks or months,
by a c——n more infamous and difhonourable (if poffible) than that ignominious p—e. If the tree is known by its
fruit, it can be a matter of little doubt,
but that the peace-maker and conven-
tion-maker are as near ally'd as the two
Sofias: the confequences then of our
celebrated p—e, and renown'd c——n,
fupported by a fortification of brafs upon
a fandy foundation, may, in a few years,
                                        prove,

prove, that, like purloin'd sheep, we may be transferred to other hands, or delivered over to the mercilefs knife of our foreign and domestic butchers, at an inconsiderable price. What share place-men and penfioners must have in such an honourable traffic, I submit to your own determination, as they are ready to obey the command of the dictator, in con-demning or approving : the ground-work of the project, you will, in a few months, find to be well cemented ; but the glory is not for you, it is for your enemies, who intend to redrefs your grievances their own way. It cannot be deny'd, but that your m——rs have ta-ken indefatigable pains for you ; that is, in scattering the feeds of difcontent at home and abroad : your colonies are neglected and made peevifh, whilft your fifter Ireland is in a ferment : but, fay they, this is caprice, humour, infolence without foundation : the deaf ear is turn'd, and their lies the redrefs of a bleeding country and broken conftitu-tion ; *but Brutus is an honourable man.*

The

The natural defence of your country
has not been fo much as thought of, for
your navy is at the loweft ebb, and the
major part of your fhips rotten; numbers of your feamen drove by neceffity
and other hardfhips into foreign fervice:
thofe at home unwilling to ferve, from
bad ufage: your foreign trade gone like
a bird of paffage; when it will return,
neither you or I can tell: the manufac-
turer and labourer ready to follow it, as
many have already done; for your taxes
are high, your poor's rates high; the
production will be mifery and famine:
no money, or at leaft very little, in the
Treafury, or to be rais'd above or under
ground; the Spaniard will take care you
fhall have none from their mines, becaufe you did not come when you ought:
he is now preparing in every quarter,
with his old relation of Bourbon, who
is as well pleas'd to fee your ruin as to
preferve his own: the fiddle-ftring of
public credit muft break; the laws and
conftitution are in a manner turn'd top-
fy-turvy, condemned murderers pardon-
ed,

ed, affaffins protected and encouraged,
thieves and public robbers conniv'd at,
and freemen, for trifling or no faults,
imprifon'd; *yet Brutus is an honourable
man.*

Place-men and penfioners will fay,
they have in no wife contributed to thefe
your calamities; believe them not; bribery being the fountain that fupports the
prodigality, infolence and extravagance,
of the greater part of them.

It is true you have laws that no place-
men or penfioners fhall be your reprefentatives: you evade thefe laws by re-
choofing them; an expedient broach'd by
your late great patriot, the grand corrupter. Pray when you are felling to
fuch candidates all that is moft dear to
Englifhmen, throw into the purchafe
your wives and children, as the wretch-
ed flaves in Africa do, that you may inherit flavery to the higheft pitch of perfection, and drop the glorious ideas of
your anceftors, who fought for *liberty,*
and

and purchas'd *freedom* with their *blood*; that it may be faid of you, what Milton expreffes in the interview between Satan Death, and Sin : " Engendering in your " bowels a fet of monfters," continually deftroying the heart of their mother country for their repaft.

Awake, then ! awake from your ftupid lethargy ! open your eyes, and be alarm'd in time at the dangers that threaten you, and which are now actually carrying on againft you, by a hellifh crew of your fecret enemies, both foreign and domeftic, in the moft private fchemes, and the moft fubtle defigns that imagination can form ; fome of which will, I hope, foon be brought to light, and laid before you.

Refolve with one common voice ; and as, " *Salus populi eft fuprema lex* ; that is, That your happinefs and fafety is the firft principle or fundamental law of the land, do not admit any man to reprefent you in your parliaments, though for the
moft

moſt venal borough, who is a place-man
or penſioner; ſuffer it not, I ſay, if you
would be free.

Were you to follow the moſt ſalutáry
advice, on this intereſting occaſion, you
would call a general meeting of freeholders in your reſpective counties, and
invite the *citizens* and *burghers,* within
each county, to attend ſuch meetings;
who, if not butchers to their country,
will attend. Reſolve, on ſuch meetings,
that no venal borough in your county
ſhall chuſe a place-man or a penſioner.
Aſk not whoſe eſtate or property the borough is, or by or with whoſe intereſt or
connections it is affected; be that as it
may, it is ſolely your's for the object in
queſtion; that is to ſay, to ſecure to
yourſelves free and independent parliaments, according to your conſtitution,
by chooſing proper repreſentatives.

Make the candidates, on every election, take the oaths on the five firſt
heads of the grand conſtitutional bill, or

fecond Magna Charta of England, which has been for fome months paft before the m——r for his perufal, without his paying to it, the proper attention it merited, and which is now in the prefs, with the national plans annexed to the bill, as laid before him : Thefe papers will, in a few days, be exhibited to the public for their information and inftruction, with interefting anecdotes touching what paffed on the fubject, which, it is not doubted, will give fatisfaction to the public, and meet their approbation, fo far as by a fteady purfuit of the national meafures laid down therein, you may be able to provide for the fecurity of yourfelves and your pofterity; in a word, of the kingdom in general, by obtaining free and independent parliaments, and thofe to be annually chofen.

Should the candidate refufe to take the oaths by the bill to be prefcribed, he may well be fufpected of a want of that attachment to the true intereft of your country, fo neceffary to be found in an

inde-

independent reprefentative; fome honeft Briton will then get on the huftings, to ferve and reprefent his country, and will comply with the terms.

Attend, therefore, in good numbers at all thefe borough elections, according to your birth-rights, to regulate and direct the mode of proceeding in fuch elections, to prevent, as far as poffible, every fpecies of bribery and corruption : for you may be eafily convinced, that the traitor (whether m——r or reprefentative) who buys you, will fell you, with the houfe of H——r in the lump, to *France*, *Spain*, or any other tyrannic *power:* in fhort, to the *power* that bids moft, when neceffity pinches, or his emoluments may be thereby enlarg'd, and his private intereft gratify'd.

Abhor, therefore, fuch men as you would a plague : do not let them approach your elections for any county, city, borough, univerfity, or cinque-port, but drive them out, as you have

done

done the wolves, from your country; your conftitution admits it, your laws confirm it, your king muft be pleas'd with it; for it is the foundation by which he reigns and governs: it is this alone can render his reign profperous, and the foundation permanent and un-fhaken.

Abolifh vice and corruption amongft yourfelves; raife public virtue once more from the languifhing ftate in which fhe droops: your country will honour the annal in which you have redeem'd, from the jaws of deftruction, the beft form'd *government* that ever was plann'd, and the rifing generation will blefs and praife you.

Begin, I fay, to work at this hydra's head, and prevent the fale of your coun-try (if it be not too late) by her fecret enemies, who are little fufpected. In purfuing thefe meafures, you will diffi-pate thofe clouds that now cover with darknefs our once bright horizon; truth
will

will then make an eafy and uninterrupt-
ed approach to the royal ear: the atrocious defigns and projects of our enemies will, nay, fhall be made known,
though propofitions for that purpofe have
been very lately with indifference treated, I fhould fay with abfolute neglect;
and thofe fchemes fo fecretly concerted
to ruin your fovereign and you, difap-
pointed and defeated. Make your king
happy, he is a *Briton*; and make him
the greateft monarch on earth, in fpite
of oppofition or mal-ad——n; for this
you can do without the affiftance of
place-men and penfioners, and none but
you can crown the work with perfection.

No grievance can come from your
fovereign, if you will be honeft among
yourfelves; he will then be great and
happy; for he knows you to be a brave
and generous people, ready to devote
your lives and fortunes for your prince,
and form'd by nature for valour, wifdom, and virtue, in the moft hazardous
enterprizes, where his honour and intereft

tereſt is in queſtion, or where your
country calls.

Avoid, therefore, as much as poſſible,
all diſſention among yourſelves, to diſap-
point your enemies, who lie on the
watch to foment them. And beware,
O freeholders, citizens, and burghers, of
the important *truſt* you have undertaken
to perform; a truſt of the moſt ſacred
kind which the ties of nature can impoſe: that is, the duty we owe our
country never to betray it. Remember
the great truſt and confidence repoſed in
you by your countrymen, to chooſe free,
independent, and unbiaſſed men for your
repreſentatives.

No place-men or penſioners are free
and unbiaſſed; therefore unfit and un-
qualified to repreſent a free people.

You impoſe on King, Lords, and
Commons, if you elect paraſites, or
murderers and deſtroyers of your country: the crime becomes your own, and
every

every punifhment that can be annexed to
it, will be but too flender. Look back
into hiftory, which furnifhes innumerable inftances of many great monarchs
being devoured and deftroyed by the
falfehood or flattery of fycophants, and
their kingdoms left a prey. By a woeful experience they have in the end
found, though too late, that corruption,
ambition, bribery, and avarice, firft
opened the door by which the paracides
entered, and brought upon them thofe
miferies they carried to the grave.

Let ftate-jobbers be afk'd, if ever they
offer to come before you again, at any
election, why, and for what, they fpend
fuch extravagant fums, and make fuch
profufe promifes, to obtain your votes,
for being your reprefentatives? and whether it be to ferve you, or themfelves,
that they difplay fuch benevolence and
generofity? Who can doubt of the latter? Even our foreign enemies are good
judges.

Had

Had our great and good *patriotic* m——rs of this century, employed half thofe immenfe fums of the public money for public utility; which they have wantonly lavifh'd in elections to corrupt voters, and fecure a majority to approve their bad meafures, and fkreen themfelves from juftice and the people's refentment; I fay, had they employ'd this public money in the fervice of their country, our fituation at this day would not have been fo defperate, nor our honour to be redeemed at the expence of fo much blood and treafure, as now becomes needful, by the daring, infolent, and unwarrantable treatment which has been lately but deliberately perpetrated, by wounding the honour of his *majefty's crown* with that of the nation, in feizing his fhips, mal-treating his officers and fubjects, plundering his effects, and infulting the flag of *Great Britain*, with impunity; acting like *pirates* in a time of profound peace; with all this and more, by a haughty, proud, and defpicable enemy.

What

What fatisfaction his majefty or the nation may receive, for fuch enormous violation of his rights, for fuch infults and depredations, will moft probably ftill be left to be determined in fome private treaty, by our kind and indulgent friends and mediators, on the other fide the herring pond, who are preparing to do much more for us, as foon as they are ready, in addition to what they have already done, and to teftify how much they love us.

The public, however, may depend on what I here relate to them, as a fact, viz. that fo long ago as July laft, on the news of the above cataftrophe, application was made by a gentleman, who had been informed of the misfortune, to a certain Lord in ad————n, praying him to give immediate orders to fit out a fleet : that foon after, feveral propofitions were made to his Lordfhip, and plans offered him by the fame gentleman, for effectually taking and reducing certain places of great importance belonging to

G the

the enemy; by which reprifals might have been then made, the Manilla ranfom recovered, with other great advantages to the nation : and the confequences of which, would, with the greateft probability, have humbled directly our haughty enemy, and produced a *chart blanche*, inftead of the wonderful convention, together with full payment of our expences, &c. But thefe interefting propofals and efforts for the public good, made by that gentleman, for the fuccefs of which he offered to pledge himfelf, and who had once before ferved the nation on a fimilar occafion, were, to his great mortification and amazement, totally neglected and unattended to; as will appear by a detail of the particulars, and the letters relative to thefe objects which will be laid before the public for their information and fatisfaction, with other curious anecdotes on the fubject.

From the foregoing digreffion, I fhall now return to my former fubject, by

faying a few words more to you, my
good friends and countrymen, with refpect to that conduct which it may be
neceffary for you further to obferve, in
choofing proper perfons to reprefent you
at your elections, as the bulwark for
fupporting your conftitution, laws, and
liberties.

Let the firft paffion you difclofe, be
that of the love of your country: examine then with a ferious attention, and
with all the powers nature has endowed
you, into the caufes of thofe grievous calamities with which you at prefent ftrug-
gle, and which threaten the almoft immediate ruin of your country; upon the
enquiry you will find, that the weight
of place-men and penfioners, againft the
unwearied efforts and labours of your
patriotic advocates, who, though hitherto in vain, ftand in the gap to defend
you, have overpower'd their moft fan-
guine endeavours, and rendered every
attempt for your happinefs fruitlefs, by
their book of numbers, in which they

exult,

exult, as if they had gained a triumph
by vanquifhing their country; fo thieves
rejoice at the defpoil of the unguarded
paffenger, till they are brought to the
Old Bailey, where they learn repentance,
when it is too late, with refpect to their
profpects in this life.

Candidates are no candidates for you,
at your elections, who will not by oath,
or the moft inviolable engagements, undertake or fwear to endeavour to reftore
the ancient conftitution to its priftine
ftrength and vigour; to impeach all de-
lin,uents and defaulters, even for fixty
years paft, to the end that their ill-got-
ten eftates, heaped upon the ruin of their
country, by their bad meafures and un-
pardonable conduct, in loading you with
unneceffary taxes, and involving the nation with a debt fhe is not able to bear;
may be, in fome meafure, fatisfied, by
a confifcation of their eftates and effects
they left behind them; in a word, to
impeach all thofe who have openly oppofed and prevented the national meafures,

fures, and honeft propofitions that have been made, for the fafety, honour, and happinefs of your country.

When you have chofen your reprefen-tatives, inftruct them, and oblige them on oath, as above, to endeavour, to the utmoft of their power, to obtain an act for annual parliaments, according to your old conftitution; by a repeal of the fep-tennial act, as alfo the act of Queen Ann, called the Qualification Act, by which rich men in land are only qualified to be chofen. This mode of choofing reprefentatives was never thought of, or fo much as furmifed, in your conftitu-tion. Your wife anceftors, knowing and forefeeing that fools and knaves were and wou'd be always found, as well among rich men in land, as among the poorer fort of inhabitants, and that wifdom, honefty, and a difinterefted love of their country, were the beft recommendations and pretenfions that men could poffefs for this important charge, never fo much as dream'd of excluding fuch perfons;

for

for if a reprefentation of the people fhould be continu'd, confin'd, and limited much longer to the landed intereft only, as it now ftands, the conftituents in time muft become flaves to their reprefentatives, and your condition as deplorable as that of the inhabitants of Poland under their tyrannic lords and mafters, call'd their nobles, to the imminent danger of your king and country, by falling into an ariftocratical government, inftead of a monarchical.

You will then chufe men of wealth, underftanding and probity; men who have a clear and juft knowledge of the true intereft, trade, and manufactures of your refpective counties, and kingdom in general : men refiding in your own counties, if poffible, who fpecifically know the peculiar interefts of their conftituents ; thefe are the men to be rely'd on ; fuch reprefentatives will bring no infamy on your choice, or any expence on government ; nor will they create faction or diftruft, to difturb the royal

ear ;

ear; or load you with unneceffary taxes, with a view to participate therein, for fupporting their luxury, pride, and extravagance; but, as honeft men and faithful fervants to their king and their conftituents, will accelerate the paffing into a law the grand Conftitutional Bill, or fecond Magna Charta before-mentioned.

As the defign of this bill is for to eftablifh national union and happinefs, to eftablifh a fuperior navy at little or no expence to the people, to reduce exorbitant and unneceffary taxes, and encreafe public and private wealth, with univerfal trade, and other popular benefits and advantages, little doubt remains but it will merit your attention and approbation, with your beft endeavours to get it paffed into a law; you will then be freed from place-men and penfioners. Locufts of every kind tarnifh the brighteft diadem, eat up the fweets of induftry, leaving the honeft farmer or labourer to withered leaves or chaff, for the fubfiftence of himfelf and his family.

Towards

Towards the more fpeedy and effec=
tually paffing fuch a bill into a law; and
as the intent and fcope of it is the happinefs and profperity of king and people, as I have before fpecified, I fhould
again recommend it to you to call a general meeting of the freeholders of each
county, to confider the advantages pro-
pofed by the bill, which if you fhould
approve, to frame an humble addrefs or
remonftrance to the throne; then inclofe
this addrefs or remonftrance to each
city and borough within each county, for
their approbation; inviting them to attend you on a day to be appointed for
another county meeting, to take the
matter once more into confideration;
then begin to fign your remonftrance or
addrefs in manner following, viz. A. B.
freeholder; C. D. citizen; F. G. burgher;
by this mode you will have the county
united in one common addrefs, which
will fhew your fovereign the fenfe of all
his people; conveying it to the royal
prefence in the ftrongeft terms of duty,
refpect, affection, and fubmiffion, that

can

can be expreffed, with your faithful and inviolable affurances of your being ready to ftake and expofe your lives and fortunes in fupport of his juft rights, againft either foreign or domeftic enemies; praying a diffolution of the prefent p———t, and a redrefs of thofe grievances which have fo loudly echoed throughout his kingdoms, to the great joy and fatisfaction of the enemies of his crown and illuftrious houfe, eftablifh'd on the throne of thefe realms, in defpite of all the combinations and confederacies, powers, fchemes, or projects, that France, Spain, and their adherents together united, could, in their diabolical machinations of invafions and rebellions, ever concert.

His royal heart, ever ready to liften, as well as to confider and relieve the juft complaints and diftreffes of his oppreffed fubjects, will weigh and reflect on his own with the national interefts, and advantages refulting from a compliance with your fupplications; for, in confi-

H   dering

dering the fubjects, (promifcuoufly or indifcriminately taken) he will find the conclufion the fame, viz. that his glory and happinefs, and thofe of his fubjects, are fo blended and interwoven together, as to become infeparable; and the objects for uniting and confirming them, invariable, if the conftitution is fupported and maintained pure and with vigour.

The wifeft and happieft of your kings have laid this precedent down as a maxim, by which they happily govern'd : hence they gain'd the hearts of their fubjects, and the command of their lives and fortunes. It has been, in following this rule, they vanquifhed their enemies, by defeating their fchemes and attempts to cultivate and foment thofe projects of difcontent and fedition among the people, with a view to depofe or dethrone the beft fovereigns that have fway'd the Britifh fceptre.

This conftitution of your's is therefore the fortrefs which defends both king and
people

people againſt all the combined powers
of the univerſe : if violated, or any
breaches made in it, the entrance will,
by degrees, in a ſhort time become fa-
miliar and eaſy ; your enemies will avail
themſelves of your folly, and overturn
your boaſted fortification ; they will poſ-
ſeſs themſelves of it by ſtorm, or per-
haps ſword in hand, without leaving you
the ſmalleſt remains of it to repair or
improve on.

Prepare then for tyranny and wooden
ſhoes, ſubmit to the yoke of ſlavery, and
bid adieu for ever to your bulwark,
which has been no leſs the admiration
and envy of all other nations, than their
dread and terror : many are the attempts
that have been hitherto made to deſtroy
it, even by ſome of our own princes,
aſſiſted by the political ſchemes and labours of France, in expending large ſums
to divide the people, and raiſe jealouſies
and diſcontents between them and their
ſovereigns, in order to introduce arbitra-
ry and deſpotic power, as the annals of

H 2   Rich-

Richlieu and Mazarine, with thofe of their fucceffors, evidently fhew : thefe fchemes, tho' fruitlefs, at length brought on thofe troubles which were fpread throughout the kingdom, in the unhappy reigns of Charles and James, and reduced thofe kings to that deplorable ftate in which their melancholy days were finifhed, without effecting their defigns; for it is morally impoffible to deftroy this glorious fhield of national defence, unlefs you put your hands to the work yourfelves, by bribery and corruption, with the aid of place-men and penfioners, who will vote away your liberties with the hopes of becoming your mafters, and afterward dictate to their fovereign, according to their own good will and pleafure : had thofe princes ftuck by the conftitution, their fate had been different.

Regard, I pray you, the heads of this grand Conftitutional Bill, the paffing of which into a law, will annihilate thofe evils, prove a *bar* to all the endeavours

that

that may be in agitation to deprive you of your freedom and independence, as well as to the ambitious views of your domeſtic or foreign foes.

Your fleets maintained without ex-pence, and deſtin'd, as therein ſpecify'd, will humble your enemies, and give you univerſal trade.

Your taxes may be, without prejudice to his majeſty's revenue, reduced, your ſeamen well provided for, and a ſufficient number always ready to man your fleets, at a call; the debt of the nation dimi-niſh'd, and other benefits to you, which will render you a flouriſhing people, and your ſovereign happy and great in your love and affections, whilſt his exchequer abounds with wealth and riches.

All this can be done, all this will be done, without inconvenience, hardſhip, or burthen on you, ſhould the bill above-mentioned take place as a law. The threats and menaces of invaſion will then
ceaſe,

ceafe, or evaporate like fmoke; without any other confequence, but, like the cries of a fkreech owl, to frighten your children, or to keep old women awake; for the empire of the feas has always been your's, and ftill muft be your's, if fleets are kept up, as I mention; fo that if our friendly neighbours fhould attempt to pay us a vifit, without your invitation, the only trouble and expence you can be at, on the occafion, will be the trouble of taking their fhips, and bringing them into port; and as to the expence, it will only be to equip them with cork jackets, and fend them back directly by the fame channel they came.

As for your inhofpitable friends Don Francifco Buccarelli, and Ignacio Madariaga, now of Falkland Ifland Dons, who, in the time of the greateft harmony and friendfhip, were fo rude as to kick us out of doors, leaving us a convention, I fhould fay a bone of contention, to exift on. Their incivility with the laws and rules of hofpitality, which they

they have violated; and the *Lex talionis*, which fhould follow, will, I find, be treated of in another publication.

True it is, that we are told we may go there again; but what fecurity have we to affure us of a kind reception, or of our quiet and peaceable poffeffion and enjoyment of what has been fo audacioufly taken from us by force; or whether, upon our arriving there, we may not meet with a more unfavourable treatment for our prefumption, than that which we received on their arrival. For my own part, I am of opinion, and I think you will concur with me in the idea, that our treatment would be rather worfe. Pray therefore your Sovereign to grant you a diffolution of the prefent p———t, and a redrefs of thofe grievances which have fo loudly echoed throughout his kingdoms, and which the enemies of his crown and illuftrious houfe have moft heartily rejoiced at.

His royal heart, ever ready to liften, as well to relieve and confider the complaints

plaints and diftreffes of his oppreffed
fubjects, will weigh and reflect on the
national interefts refulting from a compliance with your fupplications.

The world knows, that, according to the
conftitution of England, which has for
ages paft remained as an impregnable rock
againft the utmoft efforts of every foreign
power unfhaken, is nothing more than a
folemn compact between king and people,
for the mutual happinefs and fupport of
both ; it has never been violated or in-
fringed by you, nor your oaths of alle-
giance, or your attachment, ever quef-
tioned and doubted, or your integrity
fufpected, by forgetting the oaths you
have in duty and affection taken to your
lawful Sovereign, in any defection or act
of rebellion towards his crown or family.

Your Sovereign has, on his part, like
other kings his predeceffors, amidft the
acclamations and rejoicings of thoufands
of his moft affectionate fubjects, and in
the prefence of his clergy and others, in
the

the moft folemn manner fworn at the altar, in the prefence of the divine God his protector, in the words following :
" That he will grant and keep upon his
" oath, the laws and cuftoms to them
" granted (meaning his people) by the
" kings of England, agreeing to the an-
" cient cuftom of this realm, to keep
" peace and godly agreement, according
" to his power; and to caufe law, ju-
" ftice, and difcretion, in mercy and
" truth, to be executed in all his judg-
" ments."

Fear not then that your Sovereign will be difpleafed or offended at your approach, in humbly reprefenting to him the caufes of your complaints and grievances; for it is only by fuch reprefentation, and an en-quiry into them, he can fulfil his religi-ous and folemn engagement, to caufe law, juftice, and difcretion, in mercy and truth, to be rendered; and to grant and keep the laws and cuftoms granted to the people of England, by himfelf and the kings his predeceffors, by confi-

I   dering

dering your grievances and diftreffes, which you will, in the above manner, dutifully lay at the foot of his throne for redrefs.

His royal virtues are too eminently diftinguifh'd, and his religious mind but too well known to give you the leaft doubt, but that he will with patience give attention to your complaints, and maintain your rights, in preventing all encroachments made upon them and your conftitution, by a full and ample redrefs of thofe grievances you fet forth, by reftoring the old conftitution, and ex-cluding place-men and penfioners from feats in your grand affembly, as repre-fentatives of a free people; thus uniting that force, ftrength, and power of his fubjects to the crown, which forms the conftitution in its full fplendor and glory; placing the compact between king and people, on fuch ground as even earth-quakes can't remove, but which will fhake the family compact of Bourbon, overturn the bafis of that formidable
edifice,

edifice, and render the secret projects, which are yet in the hidden womb of the cursed construction, conceal'd and impenetrable, till time ripens them for execution.

His Majesty will see, by a compliance with your Remonstrance on the above matters, how easy it is to remedy your just complaints and grievances; with what ease he can prevent the discontents and divisions which are spread throughout this kingdom, and prevent, on future elections, the evil consequences attending the return of place-men and pensioners as representatives of his free people, how easily he may fill his exchequer, preserve the love of his subjects, and defeat all opposition and party faction at home, as well as the malevolent designs of his foreign enemies, to disturb his royal mind, or his lawful and rightful possessions: fear not to approach him in numbers, and enter his house in peace and humility, as you do your churches, the residence of the Almighty, whose whofe vicegerent he is on earth ; he will hear your prayers, attend to your fupplications, and grant you relief for the happinefs of his kingdoms. His own greatnefs, power, grandeur, and profperity, or thofe of his royal pofterity, are only to be found in thofe refources which flow from the hearts of a faithful, generous, brave, and loyal people ; and this, all this your Sovereign can do, by faying, I will have no place-men or penfioners in my parliament to reprefent a free people.

F I N I S.

www.ingramcontent.com/pod-product-compliance
Lightning Source LLC
Chambersburg PA
CBHW031246260626
47169CB00007B/2463